the JOURNAL OF the two Sisters

my LITTLE PONY

FRIENDSHIP is MAGIC

The Official Chronicles of
Princesses Celestia and Luna

by Amy Keating Rogers

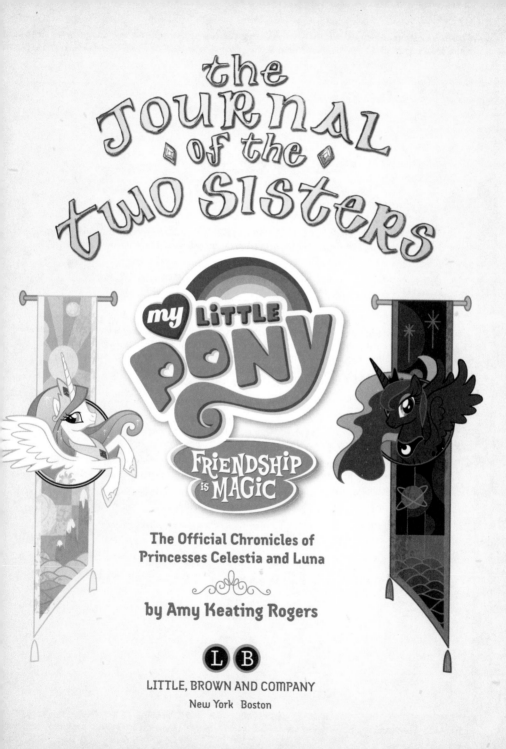

L B

LITTLE, BROWN AND COMPANY

New York   Boston

Case art by Ross Stewart
Jacket design by Christina Quintero
Jacket © 2014 Hasbro. All Rights Reserved.
Interior design by Becky James

Little, Brown and Company

Hachette Book Group
237 Park Avenue, New York, NY 10017
Visit our website at lb-kids.com

Little, Brown and Company is a division of Hachette Book Group, Inc.
The Little, Brown name and logo are trademarks of Hachette Book Group, Inc.

The publisher is not responsible for websites (or their content)
that are not owned by the publisher.

First Edition: June 2014
Library of Congress Control Number: 2014934963
ISBN 978-0-316-28224-6

10 9 8 7 6 5 4 3 2 1

WOR

Printed in the United States of America

Licensed By:

the JOURNAL of the two SISTERS

DeaR DiaRY,

My name is Celestia. Today, my sister, Luna, and I are to be crowned princesses of Equestria. I'm starting this journal so we can both write about our amazing adventures as princesses.

Well, I hope they are amazing. I don't actually know if they will be amazing. I'm assuming they will be amazing. But I guess I shouldn't assume they will be amazing because I've never been the princess of Pegasi, Unicorns, and Earth ponies. Maybe they won't be amazing. Maybe I won't be amazing. Maybe I'll be really rotten. What if I'm known as Celestia, the really rotten princess of Equestria?

Okay, calm down, Celestia. You're freaking yourself

out again. Take a breath. You're going to work hard like you always do. And as long as you work hard, you're going to be just fine. Okay. That's better.

☀ ☀ ☀

First of all, I just want to say that I can't even believe that Luna and I are going to be princesses! It all happened so suddenly and unexpectedly. A very unusual Unicorn sorcerer who called himself Star Swirl the Bearded approached us. And when I say unusual I'm not meaning to be rude, just accurate. First of all, he came by "the Bearded" quite honestly because he has the longest brown beard I've ever seen! Second of all, he wore a large wizard hat and cloak with a stars-and-moons pattern on the fabric, and all over the edging were bells that jingled and jangled when he walked. Let's just say I could easily find him in a crowd! Star Swirl and his representatives—

Smart Cookie of the Earth ponies; Private Pansy of the Pegasi; and Star Swirl's apprentice, Clover the Clever of the Unicorns—told us all about the previous struggles between the Pegasi, Unicorns, and Earth ponies. Since the tribes came to a peaceful understanding and established Equestria, they wanted rulers to help uphold that peace, which was why they came to us.

STAR SWIRL THE BEARDED

3

They knew that Alicorns stood for everything
Equestria was founded upon: love, harmony, and
friendship. And because Alicorns are a combination
of Pegasi, Unicorns, and Earth ponies, they believed
that we could represent the citizens of Equestria in an
unbiased manner—all ponies being equal in our eyes.
So they asked us to be their princesses.

And that was really nice, but still a whole lot of

pressure! I mean, Luna and I are very honored. How could we not be? It's not every day that you're asked to rule over an entire land. Actually, Luna and I clarified that our role in Equestria wouldn't be as rulers and we will not think of the ponies of Equestria as our subjects. That would be very awkward. We will be Equestria's guardians. That sounds much friendlier. We will serve and protect, watching over Equestria's lands and skies, keeping them peaceful and safe.

I just hope I end up doing a really good job and I actually have amazing adventures to write about in this journal.

CELESTia

Diary,

We are *Luna* and we are to be crowned princess of *Equestria!* Thou art our royal diary in which we shall write our most profound thoughts of being said princess and...

Oh, forget it. I was going to try to write in the *Royal Canterlot Voice*, which Celestia and I learned when we were fillies. The Alicorns thought it was an important part of our education, but we both thought speaking like that every day sounded silly. The only time we really used it was when we were playing. See, when we ran and flew in the hills of Canterlot, we'd pretend we were princesses and talk in *The Royal We*, being all formal and haughty and stuff. But as much as it's fun to speak, writing in the *Royal Canterlot Voice* is just too exhausting!

So I'm starting over. I'm Luna. This is Celestia's and my journal, where we're going to make note of the interesting stuff that happens while we're princesses. Or, as it's formally called...

The Era of the Two Sisters!
Exclamation point!

I'm going to write about the good stuff, the bad stuff, and hopefully some really awesome magic stuff, which will probably fall under good, bad, and awesome.

Today is our official coronation. And while I was excited when Celestia and I were first approached by Star Swirl and his band of merry ponies, now that it's actually happening, I'm a little nervous. I just really hope I do a good job for Equestria as their princess. I mean, it's going to be incredible, but it's also a huge responsibility!

In the end, I need to remember to be myself, and part of that is getting to know everypony and having fun! I'm excited to fly with the Pegasi, get down to earth with some Earth ponies, and whip up some spells with the Unicorns. And I'm especially excited to talk to that Star Swirl the Bearded guy again. I bet he's a great sorcerer and we could really learn a lot from each other. Plus, he has the best name ever!

Luna

Dear Diary,

Today's coronation was so lovely! Being crowned princess of Equestria beside Luna almost felt like something I'd lived before...like déjà vu. When Luna and I were fillies, we'd make tiaras out of the gems we found in the hills of Canterlot. Luna was so good at finding the prettiest ones. Then we would pretend we were princesses and fly about "our land" guiding all of "our subjects," which of course were rabbits and squirrels and a turtle named Jim. So today, as Star Swirl the Bearded placed our crowns upon our heads, it just felt like a dream come true.

Afterward, everypony enjoyed this fantastic party. The Earth ponies had grown delicious food and the Pegasi

11

had arranged the perfect weather. But the most magical moment came when Star Swirl stepped up with ten other Unicorns. Using their Unicorn magic, Star Swirl and five of the Unicorns focused their energies and brought down the sun. Star Swirl then joined the other five Unicorns, and using all their concentration, he guided them in raising the moon. It was truly amazing and took a huge amount of powerful magic. Luna and I watched in complete awe.

In thanks, Luna and I shot colorful lights from our horns, decorating the night sky. Everypony cheered in celebration. It was the perfect finale to a most wonderful day.

I don't know what I was so worried about. Everything and everypony was perfect!

CELESTIA

Dear Diary,
We art now a princess!!!

Luna ★

Dear Diary,

Because Alicorns age at a different rate than the rest of the pony races, Luna and I don't have our cutie marks yet. Being a "blank flank" at our age never felt unusual. I've always known that I would get my cutie mark at the proper time. But now that we are surrounded by so many ponies who have their cutie marks and are so much younger than we are, I must admit, it feels a bit odd.

Hopefully now that we are princesses, Luna and I will find our true calling and finally get our cutie marks.

CELESTIA

Dear Diary,

Celie and I have been touring all of Equestria, getting to know everypony and trying to decide where to build our castle. We've been flying here and there, putting on our royal princess faces, and frankly, I'm exhausted.

The question is, where do we build? It's not like every part of Equestria isn't nice. In fact, everypony is making a point of showing us just how perfect their part of Equestria is. But to be

Equestria

perfectly honest, I'd like it to be a place that's kind of away from everypony. A sanctuary. Someplace where we can have our private time. Ugh, is that a bad thing for a princess to say? Probably, but even a princess wants some downtime, right?

Anyhow, as we continued our search, Star Swirl told us about this place in Equestria called the Everfree Forest. And this place is awesome!

Everfree Forest

It's totally unlike any other part of Equestria. The plants grow on their own and the animals take care of themselves—no help from the Earth ponies! The weather does its own thing—no Pegasus assistance needed. It's just kind of... wild!

But then at the edge, there's this ravine, and deep in the ravine is this really cool tree. And, I don't know, there's just something about it. Something... magical. I just got this feeling when I saw it. I think this is where we should build our castle.

Luna

DEAR DIARY,

Luna and I were talking with Star Swirl about that tree in the ravine at the edge of the Everfree Forest, and he told us that it's not any ordinary tree. It is the Tree of Harmony! Oh my gosh! I couldn't believe it. I totally flipped! I mean, I literally flipped in the air. Luna snorted at me and rolled her eyes because I'm such a dork. But to me it was like meeting the most famous tree in the world. But that's because it's actually the most famous tree in the world!

I've read about the Tree of Harmony in books, but I didn't know that it actually existed! According to the legends, the Tree of Harmony is incredibly powerful and is said to hold the elements of all that is good and true.

It's such a fascinating tree, and I'm so drawn to it.
On it are three markings—a sun, a moon,
and a star. I've asked Star Swirl what these
stand for, but he seems to have no idea.
I don't know why, but I feel like
the sun image is calling to me.
Is that weird?

   Luna and I are both so
drawn to the Tree of Harmony
that we decided to build the
Castle of the Two Sisters above the ravine. Star Swirl
agreed, saying that having our castle built near the
Tree of Harmony would give us strength and help us
protect Equestria.

CELESTIA

Dear Diary,

Celie and I get to build our own castle from scratch. And as much as I love my sister, all she wants is for it to be a traditional old castle with arches and columns and turrets and stuff. You know what I say to that? BO-RING! Why have a regular hallway when we can have a hallway with trapdoors? Why have walls that just stand there when they can be secret doors? Normal

castle ideas

paintings? No! I want the Kind with the eyes cut
out so I can spy on ponies! Who needs plain torch
holders when they can be disembodied hooves
holding those torches? Creepy! And sure, we can

have a Throne Room. But I want a trapdoor under my throne! Yeah! Secret escape plan! Then I had this amazing idea for an organ that triggers the trapdoors, sending ponies through tunnels and plopping them outside. Not quite sure how that will work yet.

If I can convince Celie, this is going to be the BEST. CASTLE. EVER!!!

Luna

DEAR DIARY,

My sister is so weird. She wants this castle to have all these odd tricks and traps all over. And what do I really want? I want a huge library where I can finally put all the books I've been collecting all these years! Then Luna suggested that we build a secret room in the library where I could read in private! I totally geeked out at the brilliance of that! In the end, I guess we're both a little weird, huh?

CELESTIA

Dear Diary,

For the past couple of weeks, the Pegasi, Unicorns, and Earth ponies have been helping Celie and me build the castle. Things were going great, but then the most horrible thing happened. A team of ponies headed into the Everfree Forest for more supplies and didn't come back!

This was the first bad thing that's happened since Celie and I became princesses. I immediately wanted to fly into the Everfree Forest to search for the ponies, but Celie stopped me, saying we

needed to discuss things first. I guess she was right. I couldn't just go flying off without a plan. I mean, should we both search for the missing ponies? Or should one of us stay with the crew at the castle site to make sure they were safe while the other searched?

I love the Everfree Forest and have been spending any free time I have exploring it, so we decided that I should search for the ponies while Celie stayed at the castle site and kept everypony calm, easing any of their fears. Besides, we both knew she'd be way better at that than I would.

So I took off and did a sweep of the forest from above. I knew the path that the ponies have been taking for supplies, and their hoofprints had been well worn into the ground. But then they veered off in a different direction. I landed to follow, since the tracks weren't clear from the air.

It wasn't obvious why the ponies had gone this way, but all I could figure was that they needed to get supplies from a new source. Sure enough, I finally arrived where the ponies had come for supplies, but there were no ponies. I hunted around, and when I turned a corner I saw a cave that was blocked by a gate of brambles. Behind that gate I heard cries for help. It was the ponies! I ran to break them free. But before I was able to reach the cave, a huge, horrible manticore flew

at me, roaring in anger. He lunged at me furiously and I didn't know what to do. I'd never battled any pony, let alone a manticore!

I took to the air to dodge his attack, but he just came right after me, since manticores have wings, too, of course! The two of us began fighting in the

needed, came back with us to the castle site, and actually helped us build.

When Star Swirl had arrived at the castle site and heard about the missing ponies, he had feared that I would need help. I'm so glad he did! But Celie was really impressed that I discovered the truth behind the manticore's anger. Being sensitive to everypony's problems will make us even better princesses.

Luna

Dear Diary,

The castle is almost done! It's amazing what happens when you make friends with a manticore! He's strong, he can fly, and he knows every inch of that forest. Melvin (Luna said that's the manticore's name) told her all about the hidden nooks in the forest where we could get even more supplies. Plus Luna's now befriended many creatures in the Everfree Forest who have also volunteered to help. Between the ponies working in the day and the Cragadiles, the bats, and the owls working at night, we've had construction crews going around the clock.

And I have to admit it, Luna was right! While the columns and arches of the castle are lovely, her added design elements are so much fun! Though some ponies did give us weird looks when we were putting up the unusual decorations, like the paintings with no eyes and the hoof wall sconces. I don't blame them. Those things are creepy!

Today, Luna and I played hide-and-seek in the Grand Foyer. I love to duck behind the paintings, and though the Hall of Hooves still gives her a bit of a fright, the trapdoor slide is Luna's favorite. Soon the Organ to the Outside will be finished. I can hardly wait!

CELESTIA

My sister and I were
meant to rule together.

CELESTIA

Dear Diary,

You know what is the best part of building a super-weird castle with trapdoors and moving walls and a creepy organ with tunnels? I get to test it all out to make sure it works. And once I know it does, I get to mess with everypony. This is going to be so awesome!

Luna

Dear Diary,

The castle is finally finished, and today, Star Swirl the Bearded arranged a royal introduction between Luna and me and King Bullion of the Unicorns. I must say that King Bullion was very gracious to come to our castle, considering my sister and I are now taking over, so to speak. There are various kingdoms and empires that were established long before Equestria was founded. During our initial tour, we made it clear to all of them that we were not trying to step on anypony's hooves. King Bullion is still the Unicorn king of his region. As the Alicorn princesses, we are simply there to provide protection for Equestria as a whole.

While King Bullion seemed fine and quite secure in the situation, his daughter, Princess Platinum, appeared to have her tail in a twist about the whole thing. In fact, she behaved really rudely. Princess Platinum said that we had no right to be in charge of anypony if we didn't even have our cutie marks yet. She continued on, saying how <u>dare</u> we think we can rule over others if we don't even know what our true calling is? And while it's true that we still don't have our cutie marks, we have lived far longer than this arrogant princess and have been doing a fine job overseeing Equestria.

I was about to speak very rationally to the

princess on the matter, but Luna's dander was up. She really does not do well with snooty behavior, especially from somepony like Princess Platinum, who is not only far younger than her but clearly just a pain in the hindquarters. While I can't necessarily condone what Luna did, it was absolutely hilarious and practically knocked prissy Princess Platinum right out of her fancy frock!

CELESTIA

Dear Diary,

Cutting that snotty little Unicorn Princess Platinum in her place was not only deeply satisfying, but it was also incredibly fun!

Celie and I were very respectful when Star Swirl introduced King Bullion and Princess Platinum. But when our introductions were made as the princesses of Equestria, that little upstart turned up her muzzle, rolled her eyes, and claimed she didn't understand why Celestia and I were even needed. After all, <u>she</u> could have been the princess of Equestria herself. Why didn't anypony ask <u>her</u>?

I couldn't believe it. If somepony like Princess Platinum thinks she can behave that way with anypony, let alone me, she is sorely mistaken. So I busted out my loudest and most terrifying *Royal Canterlot Voice.*

"*Princess Platinum! Darest thou treat the princesses of Equestria in such a manner? We are not amused! Thy behavior is disrespectful, ill befitting of one in thy position, and reflects poorly upon the Unicorns thou art representing. Perhaps thou shalt be stripped of thy crown and thy title?*"

I expected that prissy princess to run and hide, but much to my surprise, she haughtily flipped her hair and stood her ground. Next she started calling us "blank flanks" because we don't have our cutie marks yet. Hello? We're Alicorns. There is no shame in being a "blank flank" at our age. But if she wants to get up in my business, she'd better be ready to take what she dishes out.

"Clearly thou dost not realize we Alicorns age at a different rate than other pony races. Our lack of cutie marks dost not indicate a lack of maturity. Any more than thy brandishing one means thou art actually mature."

I looked at my friend Melvin the Manticore. He was up in the balcony watching this rather heated introduction. I gave him a wink.

"With thy cutie mark, dost thou think thou could have tamed the ferocious manticore?"

And right on cue, Melvin came swooping down, letting out his most ferocious roar. In truth, Melvin is as gentle as a kitten, but Princess Persnickety didn't know that. She shrieked in horror.

"We canst not shriek in fear when our subjects art in danger! Thy cowardice wouldst have cost the lives of all the ponies in peril!"

The princess composed herself and claimed that she would have gotten her wits about her and found a way to defeat the manticore. I had to give it to her. This Princess Platinum was not willing to go down without a fight. But then neither was I.

"We see that thou art determined to sit upon our throne."

I began to back the princess up toward my throne. As I did, I looked over at Melvin and gave him another wink. He smiled and exited, knowing just where to go.

"*Fine, Princess! Let us see how thou likest the view!*"

She sat down with a beaming smile. But just as she did, Melvin hit a chord on the Organ to the Outside. The seat to the throne whipped the princess around and sent her plummeting down through the tunnel and to the courtyard of the castle. We all heard Princess Platinum shrieking. Suddenly, I began to feel really bad. Maybe this wasn't how one princess

47

should treat another princess, even if the other princess was behaving terribly.

I ran outside, and the princess was simply a mess. I felt even more horrible and was in the middle of apologizing for sending her spinning through the tunnels when she stopped me. And then Princess Platinum actually started apologizing to me! She was terribly sorry for how she had spoken to Celie and me. It was not an appropriate way for a princess... or anypony... to behave.

She said if I were willing, she'd like to start all over again. Relieved, I reached out my hoof to help her up, saying that would be really nice. As I cleaned the muck out of her mane, the princess then asked me if, as her new best friend, I could give her lessons on how to speak in the *Royal Canterlot Voice*. She thought it was simply fabulous! I couldn't help but smile.

We have a feeling
this is the beginning
of a beautiful
friendship!

Luna

Dear Diary,

   Nopony can deny that things with Princess
Platinum started out rough (funny, but rough). But now
they're going much more smoothly. When she saw how
plainly the castle was decorated, she offered to have
the Unicorns weave tapestries. Suddenly, all these
skilled Unicorn seamstresses showed up at the castle
and started weaving Princess Platinum's gorgeous
designs. She created the most beautifully elegant

images of Luna and me, and as the Unicorns hung them up on the walls, the tapestries provided that last bit of regal elegance the castle needed.

Princess Platinum even designed our official seal for the Equestrian flag to fly on the top turret outside our castle. She said she was having more flags made for all of Equestria. I'm so glad that Princess Platinum has realized that Luna and I are here for all of Equestria, including the Unicorn Kingdom, and has come around to being our friend.

CELESTIA

Dear Diary,

Today, Celestia scheduled a tour of the castle and a meeting with Private Pansy, Clover the Clever, and Smart Cookie, but I was just not in the mood to hang out with the four of them and talk about Equestria stuff. So I pretended I was sick. Then when Celestia was giving them a tour of the castle, I went through one of the secret passageways and made that tour one they will never forget!

Scaring Private Pansy was too easy. Just walking through the Hall of Hooves almost made her pass out. But then when I reached my hoof through that secret hole and brushed her on the side, she nearly hit the ceiling, she jumped so high (and those ceilings are really tall)!

Smart Cookie was a little harder to scare. That gal is a tough nut to crack. I was watching her through a painting, trying to figure out how to fluster her. But then she stood right by a fake wall. I spun it around, sending her into a totally different part of the castle. When I spun her around again, I could tell that she was shaken up.

Finally, I had to get Clover the Clever. And just like her name implies, this pony has her wits about her. Being a Unicorn trained by Star Swirl, she has magic on her

side. Every time I tried to trap or trick her, she countered it with a spell.

She was clearly aware that something was ahoof! But just like Princess Platinum, what she didn't figure on was the organ to the outside. Celestia had them all seated for their big meeting and WHAM-O! I hit the chords on the organ. Clover spun around in her seat and then went plummeting through a tunnel to the outside.

I quickly raced back to my room and got back in bed. Sure enough, Celestia came in moments later to see if I was there. She let out an annoyed "Hmmph" and left the room. Success!

Luna

DEAR DIARY,

I had a great meeting with Private Pansy, Clover the Clever, and Smart Cookie, the three representatives from the Pegasi, Unicorns, and Earth ponies who originally came up to Canterlot. Let me amend that. After Luna's high jinks—and yes, Luna, I know it was you—I had a great meeting with Private Pansy, Clover the Clever, and Smart Cookie.

They really represent these three races of ponies incredibly well. Smart Cookie noted that Chancellor  Puddinghead was making better decisions than usual, and because of this the Earth ponies were working harder than ever to produce the best crops in Equestria's history. Private

Pansy said that Commander Hurricane was calmer in leading the Pegasus Weather Brigade into action, and weather predictions were terrific. And with her mentor Star Swirl, Clover the Clever and the Unicorns were working on fantastic new spells to more effectively raise and lower the sun and moon and bring beauty to Equestria. Overall, all three of them said that since Luna's and my coronation, the sense of peace and harmony around Equestria was visible among all the ponies.

CELESTIA

Dear Diary,

Chancellor Puddinghead has to be the funniest pony I have ever met in my life! And while she has Smart Cookie to help her get things done, I think Chancellor Puddinghead knows a lot more than she lets on.

Today, she and I decided to play hide-and-seek in the castle. And you'd think that since I designed the castle, I'd have an advantage. Sadly, this was so untrue.

While I was hiding, the Organ to the Outside started playing. As soon as I heard it, I knew I was in for trouble. Suddenly, a trapdoor opened and I went whizzing through a tunnel. I landed on my hindquarters in the courtyard, where Chancellor Puddinghead was waiting. "Found you!"

I don't know how she did it, but I'm just saying that the Chancellor might just be less of a "puddinghead" and more of a "smart cookie" than ponies realize.

Luna

DeaR DiaRy,

When Star Swirl first invited us to his library, I knew it was going to be fantastic. But when I saw it, my eyes couldn't fully take it all in. The shelves were filled with ancient books and scrolls covering the history of Pegasi, Unicorns, and Earth ponies. Star Swirl also had books upon books on magic—things I had never read before. How is that even possible? Star Swirl noted that he had scrolls on everything from the Alicorn Amulet to the Tree of Harmony. Just scanning the shelves, I saw information that I hadn't even touched upon in all my years of study. Just as an example, while I've read plenty on

61

Alicorn magic, the Unicorns have their own theories and practices that differ from our ways. Amazing, right?

Star Swirl said that we are always welcome in the library: to read, research, and practice spells. I'm not sure if Luna will take him up on it, but I'm absolutely going to!

CELESTIA

Dear Diary,

Leave it to Celestia to geek out over Star Swirl's library. I mean, I want to work on spells with Star Swirl, but I don't want to sit in a big old dusty library and read through a million tomes. The two book nerds were totally bonding over scrolls and ancient manuscripts and all sorts of boring stuff. I felt like they'd given me a sleeping spell. Oh well. Star Swirl says he has an awesome spell he wants to work on with me. As long as it doesn't involve researching in the library, I'm in.

Luna

DEAR DIARY,

Star Swirl's peculiarity has made him a fantastic sorcerer. He tries things that nopony else would even dream of. He's created and mastered hundreds of spells and has so many more in the works. There's one he's developing now involving cutie marks that sounds very complex. As somepony who hasn't even gotten her cutie mark, I'm not quite sure where he's going with this spell. And honestly, it's so complicated I don't know if he'll ever finish it. But his most exciting spells involve time travel, which of course is very challenging, and the spells are causing him a bit of trouble. He has one time travel spell that can only be used once for a brief period of time. And while that's amusing, it's not really practical and certainly not what Star Swirl wants. He desperately wants to be able to travel through space and time with no limitations. I'm trying to help him with the calculations, but it's proving to be far more problematic than either of us expected. Still, we're having a great time trying!

CELESTIA

Dear Diary,

There's one area of the Everfree Forest that Melvin won't go beyond. He says it's forbidden. Well, I say that as a princess of Equestria, I need to check these things out. So I went farther into the forest, and the trees got thicker and thicker. I could barely see where I was going. The branches were scratching me. Even using my horn to light my way wasn't helping. But finally, the leaves and branches began to loosen up and I could see again.

I looked out and saw a place I'd never seen in all of Equestria. Tall grass was now under my hooves and covered the land in front of me. Terribly exhausted from walking, and not seeing anypony in sight, I took to the air to find out where I was. Suddenly, I saw a village of huts and a group of ponies down on the ground and went down to greet them. But as I got closer, I saw that while they had cutie marks, they weren't exactly ponies. They were unusually covered with stripes.

And when they saw me, they looked terribly frightened. Suddenly, they started speaking, but their language was just as different as the stripes on their coats.

"Another's come with wretched wings. What kind of evil will it bring?"

"When last one came to haunt our land, we thought we made it understand."

"Just leave us now. Desist and cease. We zebras wish to live in peace!"

"Go now! Leave now forever more! We banish you, oh manticore!"

Oh, maybe this was why Melvin said this land was forbidden. As I hovered in the air, I explained that I wasn't a manticore at all. I was Princess Luna of Equestria, and I was part of an Equestrian pony race called Alicorns. Most importantly, I did not mean them any harm. Hearing my words, the zebras calmed down. But they were still acting very wary.

"You say you fall under the Equestrian race. And clearly we have similar bodies and face. What baffles us are your wings and horn. Do all in your race get those when born?"

Understanding that if you've never seen anypony like me it might be kind of scary, I explained about all the pony races of Equestria from Earth to Pegasus to Unicorn and how Alicorn was an amalgamation of all three of these. The zebras listened very intently, clearly very wise and patient ponyfolk. I then asked what happened with the manticores, since they appeared to be afraid of them. A zebra elder stepped up and told their tale.

"Long ago, from whence you came, were horrid beasts that bore that name.

"With bodies of lions, these creatures flew. They came to hunt. Their numbers grew. Under attack, we were resigned. This was the end of zebra-kind.

"But then with potions and with spells, the zebras formed protective shells.

"The manticores could not break through. They soon grew weak and then withdrew. From that day forward, they have hidden, knowing zebra land's forbidden."

I was amazed by the zebras' tale. When the manticores grew weak, the zebras didn't attack them in return. All they wanted was for the manticores to leave so they could live in peace. I told them that I only knew of one manticore in Equestria now, and he was actually my friend. They were stunned at this. I couldn't blame them. The way things started with Melvin, I hardly thought we were going to end up as friends. Then again, if I hadn't ventured through the Everfree Forest, I would have never become friends with zebras!

Luna

Dear Diary,

I was so furious at Luna today! Well, first I was annoyed because I couldn't find her anywhere and we had a meeting with Star Swirl. I figured she was with Melvin, but when I asked him where Luna was, his eyes filled with concern. I don't understand Manticore as well as Luna, but I'm pretty sure he said their last conversation was about the forbidden area past the end of the Everfree Forest. Melvin clearly doesn't know Luna well enough to know that if you tell her

about something forbidden, she is going to want to check it out! He took me to the last place he'd seen her, at the edge of the Everfree Forest. I asked if he would help me search for my sister, but Melvin refused to go beyond this point. Clearly this area really was dangerous. So that's when I got scared for her. I told Star Swirl where I was going and that if I didn't return by nightfall with Luna, he should come searching for us.

As I pushed farther and farther into the Everfree Forest, barely able to see beyond the light of my horn, I grew more annoyed, more scared, but then finally furious at Luna. What was she thinking?

At last, I came upon a strange landscape, but I didn't even have time to take in its beauty because all I knew was that Luna was nowhere to be seen. I started flying, scanning the ground for her. Suddenly, standing in the middle of these grasslands, I saw Luna!

And she looked fine. She looked safe. I flew down, very relieved but still so angry. I immediately launched into Luna, telling her that she'd frightened me to pieces and how dare she take off without telling me and didn't she realize that I would worry about her? After all, she was my sister and the most important pony ever to me, but if I couldn't protect her, who could I protect? Finally, I stopped and realized that I was crying. And that all these eyes were looking at me. And that those eyes belonged to . . . zebras! I couldn't believe it. I'd only read about them in books! And Luna was just standing there in the middle of them.

Seeing how distraught I was, Luna ran up and hugged me tightly. Hearing about the forbidden land, she just had to go there, and then she met the zebras and got swept up in their story. But she should have told me where she was going

before she left. She was so very, very sorry.

 Relieved that my sister was okay, I calmed down and introduced myself to the zebras, who must have thought I was a little strange, flying up and yelling at my sister like that. But as we spoke, they clearly understood wanting to protect those who are close to you. I just can't believe that Luna's adventurous spirit led us to zebras!

CELESTIA

Dear Diary,

I've never really given my cutie mark much thought. As Alicorns, we were always told that when it was time for it to appear, it just would. Nothing to really concern myself about, right? But then I was hanging out with Star Swirl this evening under the stars, and he said he wanted to teach me a spell that was too powerful for him, but he was confident that with practice, I could perform it with my Alicorn magic. Eager to perform any of Star Swirl's spells, I asked what it was. "Moving the stars!" he replied with a wild gleam in his eyes. But as hard as I tried, it turns out that moving

the stars takes quite a bit of concentration.

As I was trying to focus on the stars, I became mesmerized by the moon. Star Swirl is one of the unicorns who raises and lowers the sun and moon every day, so I asked him about moving the moon. He said he'd be happy to teach me. I thought maybe once I figured out how to raise and lower the moon, I could graduate to moving the stars. Star Swirl was sure I'd be able to someday. He's such a great friend, and I'm glad he has so much confidence in me.

Luna

Dear Diary,

Star Swirl invited Luna and me over to his library today, obviously very excited to share something with us. The two of us were waiting for him for a while, when suddenly he appeared out of nowhere. Luna and I were very startled, and then Star Swirl announced with great excitement that he had finally mastered the Time Travel Spell. In fact, Luna and I had just witnessed his returning from his first trip!

Luna gave me a look and nudged me to say something to Star Swirl. I delicately said that we were very excited for him. But I was a bit surprised that he'd moved forward with the spell, because he and I had been trying to figure out the math for quite some time. Star Swirl said that he had gone through our last equation over and over and over again. He couldn't see any errors in it. "Yes," I said, "but thinking you've mastered a Time Travel Spell and actually mastering a Time Travel Spell are two very different things."

Luna gave me another look, urging me to say more. This time Star Swirl noticed and asked what was wrong. That's when I broke the news to Star Swirl that while he traveled perfectly well through time, the equation still wasn't quite correct. It wasn't just a Time Travel Spell. It was also an Age Travel Spell. Luna levitated a mirror up to Star Swirl, showing him that he was now significantly younger and only had a short brown beard upon his chin!

CELESTIA

Dear Diary,

Celie loves to fly really fast. Always has since we were fillies. And since Commander Hurricane is the fastest flyer in all of Equestria, she thinks racing with him is the best. The three of us were out today zipping through the clouds, when suddenly something with the head and wings of an eagle but the body of a lion came flying right toward us. Celie's eyes grew wide. "Griffon!" she yelled. But before any of us could react, the griffon slammed right into Celie, causing her to plummet down from the sky. Commander Hurricane and I went after Celie, flying as fast as we could to try to catch up with her before she hit the ground. The Commander caught up with her and flew her down safely. Even though the griffon had hit her really hard, Celie was just fine. But why had he attacked her?

Commander Hurricane explained that before Equestria was founded, the Pegasi and the griffons had many skirmishes over airspace. They'd finally agreed on borders, but maybe since Celestia and I had taken over as princesses of all Equestria, the griffons wanted to challenge this again. Celie and I asked the commander to take us to griffon territory to see if we could clear this up. The commander seemed very hesitant about this. But if we were to protect Equestria, we needed to keep it safe in the sky as well as on the land. Hopefully, negotiations will go smoothly and we can all fly safely again.

Luna

Dear Diary,

When Commander Hurricane, Luna, and I arrived in griffon territory, we met with Gregor, the leader of the griffons. I did my very best to kindly negotiate with Gregor the griffon, asking him to please move the griffons out of Equestrian airspace. But Gregor was grumbly, gruff, and generally a grouch. He said that the previous treaty stated that it was Pegasus airspace and that the founding of Equestria made it null and void. I stated that he was being unreasonable and that this was a technicality. However, if he insisted, all we needed to do was draft a new treaty simply replacing the word "Pegasus" with "Equestrian," and all would be well. The citizens of Equestria would stay out of griffon airspace if they would do the same with ours. But Gregor had absolutely no interest in listening to some polite Alicorn princess. He kicked us out of griffon territory and said that if we wanted our airspace, we needed to fight for it. Commander Hurricane had dealt with Gregor before and knew he wasn't bluffing. The griffons would not budge an inch. But the last thing Equestria needs is an air battle. There has to be another way. But what?

CELESTIA

Dear Diary,

The griffons are getting really bold flying into our airspace. It's actually getting quite dangerous for the Pegasi to fly. Even though he's merely been in charge of the Weather Brigade prior to this, Commander Hurricane is starting to get a defense force ready to battle them. But Celie and I really don't want a battle on our hooves. When I was speaking to Melvin, he told me that griffons and manticores are kind of similar, and not just because they both have bodies of lions. They both also have very short tempers. I noted to Melvin that I witnessed this with him and Gregor. But then Melvin let me in on a big griffon secret. They are known for having a sweet tooth. And if they don't get what they want, they can get really, really grumpy. This was totally what I saw with Gregor! But the question was, what was Gregor's treat of preference? Thanks to Melvin, I found out. As griffons flew through our airspace, Melvin joined them and found out that Gregor had a preference for pastries, specifically éclairs. Well, among his many skills, Star Swirl can whip up a batch of éclairs that will make your mouth water.

Celie and I prepared to fly back into griffon territory. But before we did, Melvin gave me one last piece of information. Back when the manticores went into zebra country, one of the things that really freaked them out was when the zebras spoke in rhyme. Now, he didn't know if griffons would be as weirded out by this as manticores, but it was worth a try. With the éclairs in our saddlebags, we flew in to propose a Griffon/Pegasus Peace Treaty. And while I had prepared the rhyme, I thought it needed a little something special to give it that ROYAL touch. Gregor flew up, and I began to speak:

"We princesses greet thee with a singular mission to deal with the gruffness of Gregor the griffon. Through Equestrian skies the griffons did choose to fly with abandon. We were not amused. Then Gregor, thy rudeness it did so offend, we could have just fought, but chose to amend. For animals, we find, do not attack when their stomachs art rumbling in need of a snack.

So Star Swirl the Bearded made your favorite éclair. Remove thyselves now from Equestria's air!"

GREGOR was visibly shaking as Celie then presented him with his favorite chocolate éclair. I'm not sure if this was because he was hungry or because he was really happy to see that éclair or because my Royal Canterlot Voice in rhyme scared the feathers off him, but upon eating it, GREGOR's demeanor suddenly changed. He apologized profusely, thanked us both for being so patient with him, and willingly removed the griffons from

Equestria's airspace, as the new treaty now
stated. Gregor also admitted that he had been a
bit cranky since his last pastry chef left. (Gosh,
I wonder why he left? Bad working conditions,
perhaps?) He also wondered if he could get
Star Swirl's éclair recipe.

Luna

DEAR DIARY,

Whenever Star Swirl travels in time, he is very careful not to tell us anything about our future. Though I can see in his eyes that there may be troubled times ahead for Equestria. I'm just so glad we have the Tree of Harmony to give us strength.

More and more, those three markings of the sun, the moon, and the star draw me in and make me feel like there is something special about them. When I said this again to Star Swirl, he got a little sparkle in his eye. For once he couldn't hide it. Those signs are important for Luna's and my future!

CELESTIA

Dear Diary,

I'm really scared. When Celie and I became princesses of Equestria, we made a promise to keep Equestria safe. And so far we've tackled some tough foes. We confronted a manticore and faced off with griffons. But I'm afraid we may not be up for what's coming. An urgent message was just delivered by a sentry of the Crystal Empire saying that Princess Amore and the Crystal ponies are in terrible danger because the Crystal Heart has been stolen!

Celie and I met the unicorn princess during our first tour of Equestria after we'd been crowned. Unlike Princess Platinum, who acted like a total pain in the hindquarters when she first met us, Princess Amore was not threatened at all by Celestia and me becoming princesses of

Equestria. She totally understood that the Crystal Empire was still her domain, but she could call on us whenever she and the Crystal ponies needed help. But nopony thought that would ever happen, because the Crystal Empire had the strongest protection of all: the Crystal Heart.

Of all the stories I heard on our travels, the one about the founding of the Crystal Empire is my favorite. See, the whole reason the Crystal Empire exists is because of the Crystal Heart. When the Crystal ponies found that Crystal Heart, the young unicorn Amore found her true calling. As a pony who was always full of love, she felt an immediate connection to the Crystal Heart. Amore projected the positive energy within her into the Crystal Heart, which then magnified that love, sending it over what would then become the Crystal Empire. Amore immediately got her cutie mark of a crystalline heart and became princess of the Crystal Empire. From that day forward, the Crystal Empire was protected by the love emanating from the Crystal Heart.

Now that the Crystal Heart has been stolen, Princess Amore and the Crystal Empire are weak and vulnerable. Celie and I must get it back. And that's what's really scaring me. Because it was stolen by...a DRAGON!!!

Luna

Dear Diary,

When Luna and I arrived at the Crystal
Empire, things were in worse shape than
we could have imagined. Without the love
emanating from the Crystal Heart, all the Crystal
ponies had completely plummeted into a state of
darkness. Princess Amore tried to send a protective
aura of love over the Empire by herself,
but without the Crystal Heart to
magnify it, her Unicorn magic simply
wasn't strong enough. She'd completely
depleted herself of her powers, and it was
unclear if they would ever be restored. We
had to get that Crystal Heart back. Maybe that could
help heal Princess Amore. But to do that, Luna and I
would have to face the dragon.

Princess Amore told us the dragon lived high up in

the Crystalline Mountain, where the Crystal Heart was originally discovered by the ponies mining for crystals. According to the legends, when the dragon heard of the amazing gems and crystals that lay within the mountain, he took up residence there, claiming the entire Crystalline Mountain as his hoard. But he had been dormant for so long, nopony knew if his existence was just a myth. The Crystal ponies began mining, and since no dragon disturbed them, they figured all was well. When they found the Crystal Heart and the Crystal Empire was born, all concerns about the dragon completely vanished. But obviously the dragon is very real, and he views the Crystal Heart as his own.

The question is: How do Luna and I convince a creature known for his selfishness to part with something that can save an important part of Equestria?

CELESTIA

Dear Diary,

I don't think I've really ever said this. Ever. But my sister is AMAZING!

First of all, we had to come up with a plan to get back the Crystal Heart. Celie thought we should try to negotiate with the dragon, which I totally got. I mean, who knows? Maybe once he knew how important this crystal was to everypony in the Crystal Empire, he'd be willing to give it back. But in case he attacked, Star Swirl prepared a powerful spell so that Celie and I could hold the dragon back. It was much more powerful than the one we used on Melvin when he attacked me. Still, dragons are incredibly strong, and I thought it was good to have reinforcements in case negotiations and magic both failed. I immediately called in Commander Hurricane, who assembled an air squad of Pegasi. I also contacted Melvin and Gregor for help. It wouldn't hurt to have a manticore and a team of griffons ready for a full-on attack in case Celie's one-on-one with the dragon went south.

Celie and I flew up to the dragon's lair with our backup close behind. We expected the dragon to be right there, guarding the Crystal Heart really closely. But he was nowhere to be seen, and the Crystal Heart was sitting right there unprotected! He'd obviously stolen it and tossed it aside, because it was sitting right on the edge of the cave like a bit of garbage. I told Celie we should just grab it and leave. But she wanted to settle things with the dragon and make sure this menace would no longer disturb Princess Amore and the Crystal Empire.

Announcing herself as the princess of
Equestria, Celie very politely requested to see
the dragon. And with a WHOOSH, he was suddenly
right in her face. He looked like he was about to
strike, so Celie and I summoned the spell to hold
him in place. It held the dragon for about ten
seconds, and then he ripped through our magical
bonds like they were tissue paper. He seemed
mildly impressed that we even tried to subdue
him.

The dragon demanded to know why we were disturbing him. Remaining calm, Celie said there had obviously been a misunderstanding. He took the Crystal Heart, which was of great importance to the Crystal Empire, and so if he could kindly return it, we would be on our way. The dragon picked up the Crystal Heart in his huge claws and held it close to Celie's face, telling her that she had a lot of nerve coming here asking for it. After all, the crystal ponies actually stole it from him when they mined the Crystalline Mountain, which was his hoard! He then looked at the assembly of flying creatures ready to battle him and merely scoffed. He asked Celie if this pathetic group was actually going to attempt to battle him if he didn't give them the Crystal Heart. When Celie said that was a last resort, the dragon snorted at her and began to toss the heart about mockingly, almost dropping it at points. It looked so tiny as he flung it about. He admitted that he <u>could</u> give it to us. After all, he had more than enough treasures. And really, this Crystal Heart was just a trifle and so terribly tacky. But, all that said, he wouldn't because he really didn't care what happened to the Crystal ponies. What was his was his, and dragons don't share. Even if perfect pony princesses ask politely.

And that was the straw that broke that Alicorn's back. Celie was willing to put on a brave face and speak with this dragon. She was even willing to battle against him if necessary. But to be spoken to with such disrespect by a creature that was simply doing something to spite others? That was something she was not willing to allow. That was when Celie pulled out the best *Royal Canterlot Voice* I had ever heard.

Suddenly, it was like Celestia was on fire! She actually glowed with fury, and her voice echoed in the air.

"How dare thee! We are not any mere pony princess! We are Princess Celestia, Alicorn princess of Equestria! We art here to protect the Pegasi, Unicorns, and Earth ponies of this land! Thou hast threatened our citizens, and we shall not stand for that! Return unto us the Crystal Heart or thou shalt pay a mighty price, dragon!"

We all looked over at the dragon, and he was shaking in absolute fear. He immediately gave me the Crystal Heart and zipped into the Crystalline Mountain. From the look of terror in his eyes, I'm sure he'll never be a problem again. Celie shook off her angry glow, becoming herself again. She didn't quite remember everything that had happened, but we all agreed that we should never make her angry.

As soon as we returned the Crystal Heart to its rightful place, Princess Amore's unicorn magic was restored, and she was able to power up the Heart once again. That energy spread all over the Crystal Empire, filling the Crystal ponies with love, which then fed back into the Crystal Heart. Everypony celebrated, inviting Celie and me to their very first Crystal Faire.

Without Princess Amore and the Crystal Heart, the Crystal Empire had been so vulnerable. Fortunately, now that the dragon is no longer a threat, they are safe, and nopony else will ever harm this perfectly peaceful community.

Luna

DEAR DIARY,

Just when Luna and I thought nothing else bad could possibly happen in Equestria, we woke up this morning to complete darkness! Well, not complete— the moon was still shining brightly in the sky, but the sun was nowhere to be seen. We were wondering who could have done such a thing when we heard the familiar jingling of bells approaching the castle. With our horns aglow, Luna and I rushed up to meet Star Swirl, but when we saw him, we were shocked. While he physically looked as young as when we'd first met him, his beard was now completely gray! We asked where he'd traveled that could have done this, but Star Swirl explained that it wasn't the time travel that caused his beard to go gray. It happened when he was trying to lower the moon and raise the sun.

As Luna and I had seen, six Unicorns are required for the task of raising and lowering the sun and moon every day and night. Star Swirl was always one of the six for both the rising and the setting. But it takes a powerful amount of magic, and what nopony told us was that the Unicorns who volunteer for the job can only withstand the task for a short period of time before their magic is completely depleted...forever. Star Swirl himself had been the only Unicorn with strong enough magic to withstand this process day in and day out, night after night. But ten other Unicorns constantly needed to offer up

their magic as a sacrifice for all of Equestria.
This morning they ran out of full-grown
Unicorns with magical abilities and were
unable to perform their task. When
Star Swirl tried to lower the moon
by himself, he was unable to, his
magic was depleted, and his beard
turned gray.

Luna and I looked at each other,
mortified. Why didn't Star Swirl come to
us sooner? Why didn't he tell us this was
happening to the Unicorns? And what could
we do to help? Star Swirl's eyes brightened. He
clearly had an idea. As we knew, Alicorns possessed
a level of magic far beyond anything a Unicorn could
ever imagine. Raising and lowering the sun and moon

wouldn't cause us any harm. In fact, if the myths he'd read were true, it would actually rejuvenate us, making our magic that much more powerful. Then, as if he even needed to say anything more, Star Swirl asked if, as princesses of Equestria, we would be willing to be the new guardians of the sun and the moon.

Luna looked nervously at Star Swirl. He'd never taught her how to lower the moon, and now that he had no magic, he couldn't! Again, he smiled. He hadn't taught her because he knew she didn't need any lessons. This was all Luna needed to hear. She and I looked at each other, and without even speaking, we expanded our wings and took to the sky. In perfect unison, I began to raise the sun just as Luna lowered the moon. It was magical and fulfilled something deep within me. I suddenly felt a sense of completion, as if I'd always been meant to do this.

I looked at Luna as we landed. In the sunlight, I saw that she now had a crescent moon cutie mark! I realized she was grinning oddly at me. When I turned, I saw that I had a sun cutie mark! We'd finally gotten them! But these were more than just cutie marks. Both markings looked incredibly familiar. I ran down to the Tree of Harmony, and our cutie marks were the exact symbols on the tree! Luna and Star Swirl had followed me. When I asked him if he knew about the pony with the last symbol of the star, he shrugged, clearly knowing something. But I guess I'll have to wait and meet that pony myself someday.

CELESTIA

Dear Diary,

I did it! I lowered the moon! Even though Star Swirl hadn't taught me, I had a feeling that I already knew how and that it was what I was meant to do. So when Celie and I woke up this morning to darkness, I thought maybe today was the day. Then when Star Swirl showed up, his words were the final boost of confidence I needed to take to the sky, meet my destiny, and get my cutie mark!

But raising the sun and lowering the moon weren't the only things Celie and I had to fix today. Poor Star Swirl's and the rest of the unicorns' magic needed to be restored. Thankfully, with all the power we'd gotten from the sun and moon, Celie and I were able to return their magic to them without any problem. Star Swirl's beard turned

brown again. Celie helped Clover the Clever, and
once I brought back Princess Platinum's magic, I
got to show off my new cutie mark. She loved it!

I've always heard that getting my cutie mark
would make me feel more complete, but I didn't
understand what that really meant until it
happened. When I flew into the sky, I knew I was
going to lower that moon to help bring on the day.
Now I can't wait until it's time to raise it again so

that I can enjoy the night. And to think that I get to do this every day and night for as long as I'm the princess of Equestria!

Luna

Dear Diary,

When Luna and I began this journal, I said that we were going to record our amazing adventures as princesses. And at first, I was afraid they wouldn't be amazing. But I have to say, from my end, they have gone beyond anything I could have ever expected.

Now that Luna and I have begun raising and lowering the sun and moon and finally gotten our cutie marks, I feel that we've entered a new stage. So hopefully, there will be even more exciting adventures to come for the princesses of Equestria!

CELESTIA

As princesses of Equestria,
we will guide and protect
all the ponies in the land.

CELESTIA

Dear Diary,

This is the first official entry of the Journal of Friendship being entered by Twilight Sparkle. Well, Princess Twilight Sparkle, I should say. And that's been a really big, unexpected change for me. I've been really nervous and feeling so much pressure. The Tree of Harmony had my cutie mark on it, and when we put the Elements of Harmony back in the Tree, it revealed this mysterious chest with six keyholes. And I've started searching, but so far, I can't find any information on how to open it or where to find these keys. But I know it's important and vital to helping me discover who I am as a princess.

Hopefully, reading the Journal of the Two Sisters will help me be less scared of this whole princess thing. After all, Celestia and Luna became princesses of Equestria and had to tackle really big problems. So if they could do it, then so can I. Right?

My friends will also be contributing to the Journal of Friendship so we can learn from one another. And maybe someday other ponies will read it and learn from our experiences as well. After all, we ponies have some really amazing adventures!

·∴✳ TWiLiGHt SPaRKLe

Dear Diary,

I'm mighty glad Granny Smith's legend about the Shadow ponies wasn't true. 'Cause I'll admit it right here and right now, I was so scared that if I'd seen or heard one more spooky thing, I woulda taken off like a jackrabbit, and Rainbow Dash woulda won Most Daring Pony. But like Twilight said, "It's good to know that whenever your imagination is getting away from you, a good friend can help you rein it in."

Applejack

3

Dear Diary,

    Just had the coolest adventure with the coolest pony ever. Came this close to blowing it because I got so wrapped up in how awesome she was, I almost forgot about how awesome I was. Good thing I didn't, 'cause it gave me a chance to show her how important it is to put your trust in somepony else.

    And I guess I never realized how lucky I am to work with a team who I totally trust. I mean, of course I handle things on my own. But being me, I've gotten into a mess of scrapes. And without my friends, those scrapes would have been a whole lot messier. Never underestimate the power of friends who always got your back.

Rainbow Dash

Dear Diary,

Rainbow Dash said I could put in a journal entry since the Cutie Mark Crusaders and I just earned the honor of carrying the Ponyville flag in the Equestria Games. But we almost didn't because I was too focused on myself instead of all of us as a team.

See, what makes Ponyville so special is that it's a place where Earth ponies, Unicorns, and Pegasi live together as friends—like Apple Bloom, Sweetie Belle, and me! But when I got it in my head that I wasn't a good Pegasus because I couldn't fly, things got all messed up. All I could focus on was trying to fly instead of realizing that our routine was awesome already and the abilities I had made it that awesome. I just couldn't see it that way. I thought I didn't matter because I'm . . . different.

   The thing is, being
different and not being
able to fly aren't bad
things. It's part of who
I am! Plus, my friends
love me for the pony I
am now, not for the pony
I could be in the future.

That's real friendship. So I was awfully silly to
run away from my teammates when they would
stand by my side no matter what.
                   And now we'll be standing
                   by each other's sides as we
                   carry the Ponyville flag into
                   the Equestria Games!

friends
forever

                   Scootaloo

SPIKE

Dear Diary,

Sweet Apple Acres almost had its lifeblood of apple juice sucked right out thanks to this pony bein' shortsighted with a short-term solution. Why, when vampire bats threatened our orchard, this pony couldn't see the forest through the trees. My good friend Fluttershy thought of the needs of

the critters, sayin' we should give 'em a piece of our land and that, in fact, the bats would make our future crops even better. Leave it to this pony to be stubborn as a mule! I didn't want those varmints anywhere near our apples or our land! So we made Fluttershy go against her good nature and put the

STARE on them creatures so Twilight could cast a spell on them, sucking away their vampire ways. Well, we were the ones that ended up gettin' bit 'cause that there spell turned our sweet friend into the biggest vampire bat of them all! Just goes to show you should never let anypony pressure you into doin' something you don't think is right. And when one of your closest friends tells

you no, you better pony up and accept it because nothin's worth jeopardizin' a friendship.

Applejack

Dearest Diary,

   Manehattan was simply grand. It was in this magnificent metropolis that I learned that while there are ponies who will take advantage of your generosity, you should never, ever let that cause you to abandon your generous spirit. Nothing feels worse than taking advantage of the giving nature of your friends.

   After all, it is my friends who pulled me through this debacle. It is my friends who generously gave up their time and all their plans and helped me receive the accolades of all the fashion industry. I was swept up in the cold, callous world of Manehattan, thinking that was all that mattered. But when my friends weren't there to share in my success, I realized that this success was the last thing that mattered. Realizing I'd treated them so horribly—it just wasn't worth it. I never want to be that kind of pony!

Why, it may be "everypony for herself" in the big city, but this small-town filly is just fine being the generous pony she's always been—though a little bit wiser and more cautious than she was before.

Rarity

Dear Diary,

I've learned so many facts about Star Swirl the Bearded and have studied so many of his spells. So why didn't I realize that Star Swirl would have known Celestia and Luna? After all, on Nightmare Night, Luna commented on my costume and said that I got the bells right on my cloak. Star Swirl let Celestia visit his library, and Luna did spells with him at night! Star Swirl was their friend! That is so cool!

TWILIGHT SPARKLE

Dear Diary,

Families are super. Super complicated, that is! Just take my sister. She can be a bit of a bossy pony, but that's only 'cause she wants what's best for everypony. And Big Mac is the best brother, but the fella's gotta speak up now and again! And I love me some Granny Smith, except when she makes me wear some silly old bonnet. But, honestly, family is awesome 'cause you can be goin' on some borin' old road trip, and as soon as you "accidentally" lose the map, that's when the real adventure begins!

Apple Bloom

Dear Diary,

   Four core and seven seeds ago, the Apples came to this here land ready to kick up some dirt and make our gardens grow. And the Apple family grew as strong as the roots of any apple tree, diggin' deep into the soil and feeding off the nutrients of the earth. But just as different apples have different flavors, different Apple ponies have different personalities. And even though we're family, even Apples can work your last nerve and make you fit to be tied! That's when this old pony remembers that we're Apples to the core and at the center of that core is love. And a whole lot of butter.

Granny Smith

EEYUP!
Big Mac

Dear Diary,

I know that the Apple family is the best family ever. But I thought that bein' the best family meant bein' perfect. And everypony knows that while we love our family, the last thing families are is perfect! What truly makes a family the best is bein' able to get through them rough patches together. The best families are able to forgive each other's mistakes, 'cause goodness knows we all make plenty of them! Through thick and thin, you've got your kin! I feel mighty lucky, 'cause some of my best friends are my family. But what makes me a might luckier than that is that I've got such good friends, they feel like family, too.

Applejack

Dear Diary,
    i LOVE THiS FAMiLY!!! BEiNG AN APPLE iS THE MOST AWESOME THiNG EVER!

Pinkie

Dear Diary,
    I must admit that I'm a little nervous about the Equestria Game trials that are coming up soon in Rainbow Falls. Rainbow Dash is so looking forward to them, and she so desperately wants our team to qualify; I would hate to disappoint her. I just hope she knows that, no matter what, I really tried my very best because she's my good friend and I would never do anything to betray her.

Fluttershy

Dear Diary,

Training with Spitfire and Fleetfoot for the Equestria Games was totally awesome. I mean, they're Wonderbolts and really know their stuff when it comes to flying. And when they asked me to fly with them as part of Team Cloudsdale, I gotta say, I was totally tempted. But then there's Fluttershy and Bulk Biceps from Team Ponyville. They may not be the strongest flyers—well, let's face it, they're not the strongest flyers—but they sure get an

A for effort! And they represent the home team of Ponyville. And as Pinkie says, "Pee for Ponyville."

Still, I can't deny it, I LOVE to win...really, really love it. But if I ever gotta choose between winning and being loyal to my friends...I'm always gonna choose my friends. 'Cause as much as I love winning, I love them waaay more!

Rainbow Dash

DeaR DiaRY,

All I wanted out of today was a nice relaxing day with Cadance. After all, the two times we were together, things hardly went smoothly.

Her wedding to my brother? She'd been trapped at the bottom of the castle and was being impersonated by the changeling queen. My visit to the Crystal Empire? King Sombra

18

attacked! Just once I'd like to have a day with Cadance when the fate of Equestria wasn't hanging in the balance.

And I had such a great day planned! The Star Swirl the Bearded Traveling Museum was in Ponyville for one day only! What could be better than spending the day with my best friend/sister-in-law combo while looking at Star Swirl the Bearded artifacts, reading his old manuscripts, and seeing which of the bells from his cloak was on display? Totally the best day ever!

That is, until Discord showed up with his "Blue Flu," mucking up all my plans to try and have a nice mellow day with Cadance. And it wasn't bad enough that we had to play nursemaid to his fake illness. He sent us on a wild-goose chase to the ends of Equestria for a remedy and had us battling Tatzlwurm. On the one day when the fate of Equestria wasn't in our hooves!

I think it's pretty clear that my visit with Cadance didn't go quite the way I expected. But in the end, I realized that when you're with a good friend, even the most chaotic day can wind up being a great experience that brings you closer.

TWiLiGHt SPaRKLe

Dear Diary,

It's good to be proud of what you do. Like, i'm really proud of making everypony smile and laugh and planning the best parties ever! But when my pride got in the way of hearing Rainbow Dash laugh at her own birth-aversary, i knew it was time to retire the old party cannon. 'cause if it was a choice between forfeiting a competition to be the bestest party planner ever or getting to hear my friend laugh again, i will choose hearing my friend laugh again, hooves down! Fortunately, i didn't have to choose! Together, cheese Sandwich and i threw a totally epic party for Rainbow's tenth birth-aversary! And i've never been more proud!

Pinkie Pie

Dearest Diary,

I was ever so excited to execute my vision for the Ponyville Days Celebration. Small-Town Chic was going to be the greatest theme and such an expression of who I am. I put so much time, effort, and thought into the planning of it all. And I desperately wanted Trenderhoof to be impressed, but not just with the party. With me.

So when I saw that he was more interested in a simple farm pony like Applejack, not only did I change the theme of the Ponyville Days Celebration, I also went about changing myself. And I did it all to impress this pony and try to get him to like me, which is terribly silly and never a wise choice.

Organizing the Ponyville Days Celebration was one of the hardest things I've ever done, but I learned an important lesson. Real friends will like you for who you are, and changing yourself to impress them is no way to make new ones. And when you are as fabulous as I am…it's practically a crime.

Rarity

Dear Diary,

is this a place where we can just plop down our random thoughts? Good, because i have plenty of those. i mean, i could fill my own book and call it

"Pinkie's Random Thoughts."

So for today's entry, i would like to tell you about a phrase that i thought was a word. i'm guessing that you don't know it because you are a book. But then again, books are filled with words and phrases, so maybe you read yourself and learned this word/ phrase and i'm just telling you something you already know. But i'm guessing you don't, and since you're a book where we're supposed to be writing down useful and informative information, here i go, being both useful and informative.

The phrase is "slippery when wet." i heard this phrase a lot when i was a little filly growing up on the rock farm. See, when rocks get wet in the rain, they are "slippery when wet." That's what my sister Maud always used to say to me.

"Slippery when wet! Slippery when wet!"

And no truer thing was ever spoken! i slipped on more slippery rocks on that rock farm than i can remember. Actually, that's not true. i remember each and every one. There were 4,745. Those rocks really were "slippery when wet"!

The thing is, and this is the important part of my lesson, Diary, i didn't realize that "slippery when wet" was a phrase. i thought it was one big word:

slipperywhenwet.

And i thought it meant really, really, really, really, really, really, really, really, really, really, really, really, really slippery. i would add 4,733 more "reallys," but that's going overboard, don't you think? Every time it rained on that rock farm, i thought, "Slipperywhenwet, slipperywhenwet, slipperywhenwet."

Every time i tried to walk safely inside past the rocks, i thought, "Slipperywhenwet, slipperywhenwet, slipperywhenwet." And every time i slipped on the rocks and fell, i'd think, "Ouch."

26

It was only later when i moved to Ponyville that i realized that "slipperywhenwet" was actually "slippery when wet," and it's all thanks to my friends. See, Rainbow Dash was making it rain in Sweet Apple orchard and Applejack told her to be careful of some rocks, 'cause as Applejack noted, "if you hit them there rocks with the rain, they're gonna get all slippery when they're wet."

No truer words were ever spoken! Well, except,

"NEVER EAT ONE HUNDRED CUPCAKES IN AN AIR BALLOON WHEN RETURNING FROM CLOUDSDALE IF RARITY IS WEARING A BRAND-NEW FROCK THAT SHE DOESN'T WANT COVERED IN CUPCAKES WHEN YOU SUFFER FROM FLIGHT SICKNESS."

i learned that one the hard way!

My point, Dear Diary, is that I finally realized that "slipperywhenwet" actually meant "slippery when wet." And it's a good thing to note as you go through life. Well, not you, Diary, 'cause you're a book and you won't be slipping on things when they get wet. In fact, you won't even get "slippery when wet." You'd just get soggy when wet! Ooh!

Don't get wet, Diary! Stay dry!

But now that I'm thinking about it, not everything gets "slippery when wet." Mud gets goopy when wet. Sand gets sticky when wet. And water just gets more wet when wet.

Well, Diary, this is food for thought. Speaking of which, I'm hungry. I think I'll let you ponder everything i've written here while i get a snack. i'm really in the mood for some of Granny Smith's apple-spice muffins. Yum! Hope you enjoyed my latest entry in "Pinkie's Random Thoughts."

Oh wait! This is the Journal of Friendship! Oops! Um . . . hey, friends . . . rocks get "slippery when wet," which can also mean "slipperywhenwet," which means really, really, really, really, really, really, really, really, really, really, really, really slippery. Plus 4,733.

So WATCH OUT!

Pinkie

Dear Diary,

I don't know if you know this, but I'm terribly shy. It's true. I don't like to speak up. Or say things. Or be noticed. Or have everypony's eyes on me. Or draw attention to myself. Or contradict somepony. Or cause a ruckus. Or be a bother. Or be the standout in a crowd.

But I do love to sing. Oh goodness, it makes me so very happy. But it's not something I would ever, ever, ever want to do in front of everypony. That would be the most frightful of frightful things. Even worse than staring down a dragon! So I've only sung for my animals in the privacy of my own home, where I feel very, very safe.

Then I accidentally discovered something I never, ever expected. Not only do I love to sing, I love singing in front of everypony. I love hearing their applause and their praise. I actually love to...perform! But I was too scared to do this in my true voice in front of everypony, so I had to use a false one while hiding. And that's so very silly.

Sometimes being afraid can stop you from doing something that you love. But hiding behind these fears means you're only hiding from your true self. It's much better to face those fears so you can shine and be the best pony you can possibly be!

Fluttershy

Dear Diary,

Well, I guess Twilight must not be so super upset anymore 'cause she's letting us do a diary entry like our sisters do. Boy, did we get our priorities so mixed up. We started acting special because we were friends with someone special. We almost forgot the real reason she's special: because she's our friend. But she forgave us, and like magic, things are as good as new. That's the kind of magic I really want to get good at...now that I'm getting so good at the other kind. We're just glad Twilight Time is back to normal.

Sweetie Belle

Dear Diary,

The Breezies were adorable, and I really didn't mean to throw them off their path! It was ONE leaf!! Just because they're tiny and super adorable doesn't mean that they're immune to accidents like the leaf that I never should have crossed paths with!

SPIKE

Dear Diary,

My instinct is always to nurture those in need. I feel the urge to help others when they are in a bad situation, especially the cutest of creatures. Telling somepony no seems so mean, goes against my nature, and feels like it's the opposite of my Element of Kindness.

My experiences with the Breezies have helped me to see that kindness can take many forms. Sometimes being too kind can actually keep a friend from doing what they need to do. Pushing them away may seem cruel, but it is sometimes the kindest thing you can do.

Fluttershy

Dear Diary,

I cannot remember a day when I wasn't Apple Bloom's big sister. Why, it's been my job to protect that little filly and keep her safe since the day she was born. That's a job that never gets scratched off my checklist because it's not a chore; it's an honor.

So it's mighty hard for me to pony up to the fact that this little filly will have her cutie mark before I know it and soon be lookin' me square in the eye when  we're buckin' apples. But after what I've seen today, I realize that perhaps I've gotten a bit overprotective and been babyin' her a bit much. In fact, I think it's high time for me to loosen the reins on Apple Bloom. Still, she will always be my baby sister.

Applejack

Dear Diary,

Sometimes, one of your best friends wants you to bond with another one of their best friends. But when you meet that friend, you realize you have nothing in common with that pony besides that mutual friend.

The girls and I couldn't have had less in common with Pinkie Pie's sister Maud. No matter how we tried, there was just no connection, and sadly, she felt the same way. The worst part was, by not being friends, we were all breaking our best friend's heart. Talk about being between a rock and a hard place!

But when we finally realized that Pinkie's happiness meant as much to us as it did to Maud, that was all we needed in common to bring us together as friends. For the love of Pinkie.

TWILIGHT SPARKLE

Dear Diary,

Well, I guess I have another entry to write, don't I? Having a big sister who steals your spotlight can get really frustrating. Especially if that sister is so amazingly talented that she seems to outshine everything you try to do to make yourself stand out and be special.

I thought I had it bad with my sister Rarity, but nopony understands this better than Princess Luna, and she taught me an important lesson. She showed me that my jealousy over Rarity's talents could really destroy her future. I'm just lucky that I have a sister who's also my friend and that friends forgive each other. As Princess Celestia so perfectly said to Princess Luna, "It's wonderful when sisters can work out their differences, is it not?"

Sweetie Belle

Dear Diary,

Seeing Granny Smith makin' a splash and kickin' up her hooves woulda made me pleased as punch. The only hitch in the giddyup was that Granny had it in her head that she was healed of all her aches and pains thanks to Flim Flam's Miracle Curative.

The bigger hitch was that I played along, not tellin' her the truth. And the longer I didn't tell her, the bigger the lie became. Soon Flim and Flam had roped me into a heap of lies, and I just don't cotton to that. Once you've told the lie, how do you pony up and tell the truth?

Being honest sure gets hard

when it seems like the truth might hurt
somepony you care about, but I think
believing a lie can end up hurting even
more. Maybe someponies don't care about
that, but I sure ain't one of them.

Applejack

Dear Diary,

Rainbow Dash finally learned the history of the Wonderbolts, but she's not the only pony who needed a lesson. I needed to learn something just as important. The fact is, different ponies learn differently. Some learn through song, others through visuals...and while I am a "sit and learn" pony, I had to put aside my hard-and-fast rules of learning to discover that Rainbow is a "fly and learn" pony.

One way of learning isn't better than another. Having a different technique certainly doesn't make you dumb. After all, everypony is unique and individual!

TWiLiGHt SPARKLe

Dear Diary,

I was so frustrated having to learn all those dates and old pony names and historical places for the test on the history of the Wonderbolts. I mean, sure, it was kind of interesting to know that General Firefly assembled the awesome flying team called the Wonderbolts. But the costumes? Why did I need to know about goofy, silly costumes? Did I need to know that General Firefly's was itchy and unattractive?

Ooh! I still remember that! Awesome!

Still, at first I didn't see why I needed to know any of that stuff to become a Wonderbolt. Isn't it enough that I'm the most amazing flyer ever?

Then I realized that Twilight's kind of right. It's a really big deal to be chosen as a Wonderbolt. An honor and a privilege. So knowing that history is actually a really big deal, and I'm glad I finally know it. Now if I'm chosen, I can represent all those who came before me, flying proud as a Wonderbolt.

Rainbow Dash

Dear Diary,

Gosh, I really did want that book. A lot. It was worth more to me than a pin, or a chalice, or an antique chicken, or an Orthros. And I even said I wanted that book more than anything in all of Equestria. And I meant it. But there's nothing in all of Equestria that's worth as much to me as a friend. I mighta forgotten that for a little bit, but it's true. Which is why there was no way that trade could be fair.

I'm just glad I finally realized that before it was too late. Before I lost one of my very best friends. And I'm glad that Daring Do collector called off the trade, because sure, I woulda been the only pony with a complete set of all the Daring Do first editions. But I also woulda been a pony with an incomplete set of friends. And my friends aren't just first editions. They're one of a kind.

There were hundreds of ponies trading everything from diamonds to dog collars. But no matter what any other pony traded for, nopony walked out of there with anything more valuable than us, 'cause we left with our friends.

Rainbow Dash

Dear Diary,

The Equestria Games were so amazing. I guess. I was too busy being hard on myself to really enjoy them. As soon as I showed up at the Crystal Empire, everypony was treating me like I was this big hero because I saved them from King Sombra when I carried that Crystal Heart. And since they felt I was a hero, I felt like I had to live up to it.

They asked me to light the torch for the Opening Ceremony. Which shoulda been a cinch, right? I mean, I'm a fire-breathing dragon after all. But when the time came, I totally choked. Literally. I couldn't even muster up a spark! And what was even worse, Twilight had to light it for me with magic! After that, I got it so stuck in my head that I had to prove myself to everypony that I just kept messing things up more and more.

Thank goodness, when everypony was actually in danger, I stepped up without even thinking about it. I breathed fire and actually saved the day. But that wasn't good enough for me. I mean, that's exactly what anypony or anydragon else would have done if they could have, right? If their magic wasn't being blocked or if they could breathe fire like me. Everypony kept trying to convince me that I was great.

You know, it's weird…no matter how many times others tell you that you're great, all the praise in the world means nothing if you don't feel it inside. And when you care about doing things well, you can become your own toughest critic.

Sometimes, to feel good about yourself, you've got to let go of the past. That way, when the time comes to let your greatness fly...you'll be able to light up the whole sky.

SPIKE

Dear Diary,

Reading all about Celestia's and Luna's early years as princesses has been both enlightening and discouraging. While I have my friends, Celestia and Luna only had each other. Yet they managed to keep everypony in Equestria safe. With just the two of them, Celestia and Luna befriended a manticore, negotiated a truce with the griffons, and even scared a dragon! And what's my biggest worry? How to open this magical chest! I've been searching everywhere, but I still haven't got a clue.

If I can't figure out where to find these keys, what kind of princess am I going to be?

TWiLiGHt SPaRKLe

Dear Diary,

♥♥me again! ♥ And today was Lollygabbing Day. Wanna know what that is? Yeah, i bet you do! Lollygabbing Day means that today i did absolutely nothing EXCEPT talk about absolutely everything! Best day ever, right?

Well, i thought so, but it seems like not all my friends were as up for Lollygabbing Day as i was. When i told Twilight it was Lollygabbing Day, she tried to correct me, saying the word is "lollygagging," not "lollygabbing." Well, that's because i made it up! i took the word "lollygagging" and the word "gabbing" to make a whole new word: "lollygabbing." it's a combo!

Twilight gave me a funny look—has she ever given you that funny look,

Diary? Then she pulled out a very fancy-schmancy calendar and said that "Lollygabbing Day" was not an official day on the calendar of Equestria. Well, i said, that may be so. But who decides on those officially named days? Huh? is it, perhaps,

princesses? Hmmmmm?

What if some ordinary pony wanted to have her own special day? What makes that day any more or less important than the Running of the Leaves or Winter Wrap-Up? Or...or... even the Summer Sun Celebration! Yeah!

So i grabbed that fancy-schmancy calendar, and with the stomp of my hoof, i, Pinkamena Diane Pie, officially dubbed today Lollygabbing Day! Well, Twilight wasn't very happy that

47

i stomped my hoof on her fancy-schmancy calendar. Especially since i had frosting all over it from eating my Lollygabbing Day cupcake for breakfast earlier this morning. So i high-tailed it out of there while she was still speechless. But i did tell her that after i was done lollygabbing, i'd be here at the castle when she was done with her important stuff, like trying to figure out how to open that magical chest and cleaning the frosting off her fancy-schmancy calendar.

Next, i tried to lollygab with Applejack and Rainbow Dash and Fluttershy and Rarity, but the funny thing was everypony seemed too busy to lollygab. i ask you, Diary, what kind of world do we live in where one day a year ponies can't

just lolly and gab all day long? i'll tell you what
kind of world, Diary—a world that
needs a lot more

Pinwheels and Piñatas.

But i digress. Since my
friends were too busy to
lollygab, i invited them all to come
here when they were done with all
their apple bucking, cloud kicking,
critter tending, and clothes
making.

i lollygabbed all around Ponyville, and
you know what, Diary? i can talk about just
about everything when i'm doing absolutely
nothing. candied pecans, umbrella stands,
hoof buffers, balloon puffers, party
streamers, my left femur. The list
is endless. But believe it or not, i was
finally all talked out. So i came here.

And having lollygabbed every little thing out of my head, all i wanted to do was just sit here in this creepy old castle in silence.

You know what happened, Diary? My friends showed up! And you know what they wanted to do? They wanted to talk! They wanted to blab! They wanted to blather on! They wanted to... lollygab! Yep, seems that once i was gone, they realized how quiet things were without me, and so now they wanted to lollygab with me!

Well, excuse me, but did they not see me sitting there silently meditating? Hello? Trying to have a zen moment here!

My friends felt really bad and started to leave the castle with their heads hanging low. i know this because i was peeking out from the corner of my closed, meditating eye.

Then I figured that was a long enough moment of silence.

Let's get back to Lollygabbing Day!

And that's when Twilight showed me her fancy-schmancy calendar. On it there was a mark (that I think was still part frosting) showing that today was now OFFICIALLY Lollygabbing Day!

Pinkie

Dear Diary,

I would do absolutely anything for Rarity. I mean, she called me her <u>favorite</u> dragon! And when she said that I was one of her dearest and most supportive friends, I just had to find a way to help her when that puppeteer Claude was such a...a...clod! I had to help her get her creative spirit back. That Inspiration Manifestation Spell sure did the trick, but it didn't really help Rarity, and I was too afraid of hurting our friendship to tell her.

But today I learned how important it is to be honest with your friends when they're doing something that you don't think is right. A true friend knows that you're speaking up because you care about them.

 SPIKE

Dear Diary,

Once again, the Magic of Friendship and the Elements of Harmony have proven to be the solution to the most challenging and horrible threats against  Equestria. And while I've been scouring for hints in every book and scroll on where to find the keys to open the chest, it turns out that the clues were right here in the Journal of Friendship!

I didn't discover this on my own. Discord read our Journal of Friendship and highlighted specific entries. In each of them, my friends faced a difficult choice, but they remained true to themselves and embraced their Element. In turn, this helped another pony make the right choice in her life. Because of this act, each of my friends was then given an object, or key, from the pony whose life they helped change.

That meant five keys. We needed <u>six</u> to open the chest, but I hadn't yet been faced with my difficult choice where I had to embrace my Element. That is, until Tirek threatened Equestria and Discord betrayed us all by joining forces with him. Because of that betrayal, Tirek was going to destroy all of Equestria and all my friends.

When I had the choice of giving up the combined Alicorn magic of Celestia, Luna, Cadance, and myself or freeing my friends, I chose my friends—including Discord, the one who caused all this with his betrayal of his friendship to us. By being a friend to Discord at a time when it wasn't easy, I embraced my Element, the Magic of Friendship. Seeing this act of Friendship, Discord then gave me a medallion as a sign of his true friendship.

With that final key, Rainbow Dash, Applejack, Rarity, Pinkie Pie, Fluttershy, and I were finally able to open the chest and unleash the Magic of Friendship! Together we defeated Tirek and restored Equestria and all its ponies!

The other issue I've been struggling with, Journal, is who I am and what I'm supposed to do now that I'm <u>Princess</u> Twilight Sparkle. I mean, am I just supposed to smile and wave at everypony? Isn't there supposed to be more? Well, I'm happy to say that the answer is YES! When my friends and I unlocked the chest, a beautiful, sparkly, and colorful castle was revealed.

(Seriously, Rarity is beside herself.)

Through this experience, I proved that the Magic of Friendship is always with me, and I have the power to spread that magic across Equestria. That is the role I am meant to have in our world. It is the role I choose to have as the princess of Friendship!

What's wonderful is that I don't have to take on that task alone. I will have my friends by my side. Our new role in Equestria may change a few things, but it won't change the most important thing:

the Magic of our Friendship!

♥

Princess Twilight Sparkle, the Princess of Friendship

*Use these pages
to write about
the magic in all
your friendships!*